MW01610546

ADAM
in
Lost and Found

Zanib Mian
ILLUSTRATED BY
Maria Mian

Muslim
Children's
Books

For Abdurrahman, who always does
what's right
-Z.M

For my earthy, wild child, Elias
-M.M

First published in Great Britain in 2012
Published in this edition in 2022
by Muslim Children's Books

**MusLim
ChiLdren's
Books**

www.muslimchildrensbooks.co.uk

Text © Zanib Mian 2012
Illustrations © Maria M. Goncalves 2012
The right of Zanib Mian and Maria M. Goncalves to be identified as the
author and illustrator of this work has been asserted by them in accordance
with the Copyright, Designs and Patents Act, 1998.

A CIP copy is available of this from the British Library.
ISBN 978-1-9160236-8-0

Adam and his family were on a train, on their way back from visiting aunty Fatima in Manchester. Adam **loved** trains! He loved how the doors whooshed open; he loved how fast they were; and best of all, he loved the noises they made.

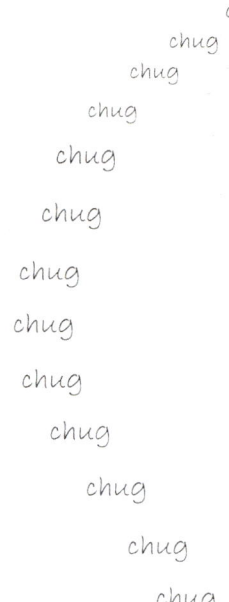

chug chug chug chug chug chug chug chug chug chug chug chug chug chug chug chug chug chug chug chug

whoosh

London

zooooooooooooooooooooooooooooooommmm

Adam looked at the toy plane in his
hand. He took it everywhere with him.
It was his absolute favourite.
Mum had even **carved** his name onto it.

But he wished he had a toy train.

"Come on," said Dad,
"Time to get off the train."

Just then, Adam saw something
shiny and red
He went to get a closer look.

It was a toy train!

As they stepped off the train
and joined the crowd of people,
Mum asked,
"What's that you have there, Adam?"

"It's a train!
I found it!
Finders keepers losers weepers!"
said Adam.

"Twain twain!" shouted Zacharia.

Dad said everyone should sit on the bench and talk about the train. Mum and Dad wanted Adam to give the train to the lost property man.

"A little child has lost that train, Adam, and he will be very upset if he can't get it back." said Mum.

"But I like it... and I found it" Adam said.

Mariam said Adam was being a selfish little boy.

Dad explained that if Adam did the right thing, Allah would be pleased with him and give him a *good reward.* But if he didn't, he would have to tell Allah one day why he kept something that wasn't his to keep.

Adam closed his eyes and thought **very hard.**

"OK," he said, "I **ABSOLUTELY** want to give it to the lost property man."

Mum gave him a warm hug.

Later, when they were home,
Adam looked in his rucksack
for his toy plane.

BUT IT WASN'T THERE!

Adam was very sad.
Mariam said she
would help him look
everywhere for his plane.

"Let's look between
the sofa cushions!" Mariam said.

It wasn't there.

But they did find
A DRIED UP HULA HOOP,
A LOLLIPOP,
AND A FIVE PENCE COIN.

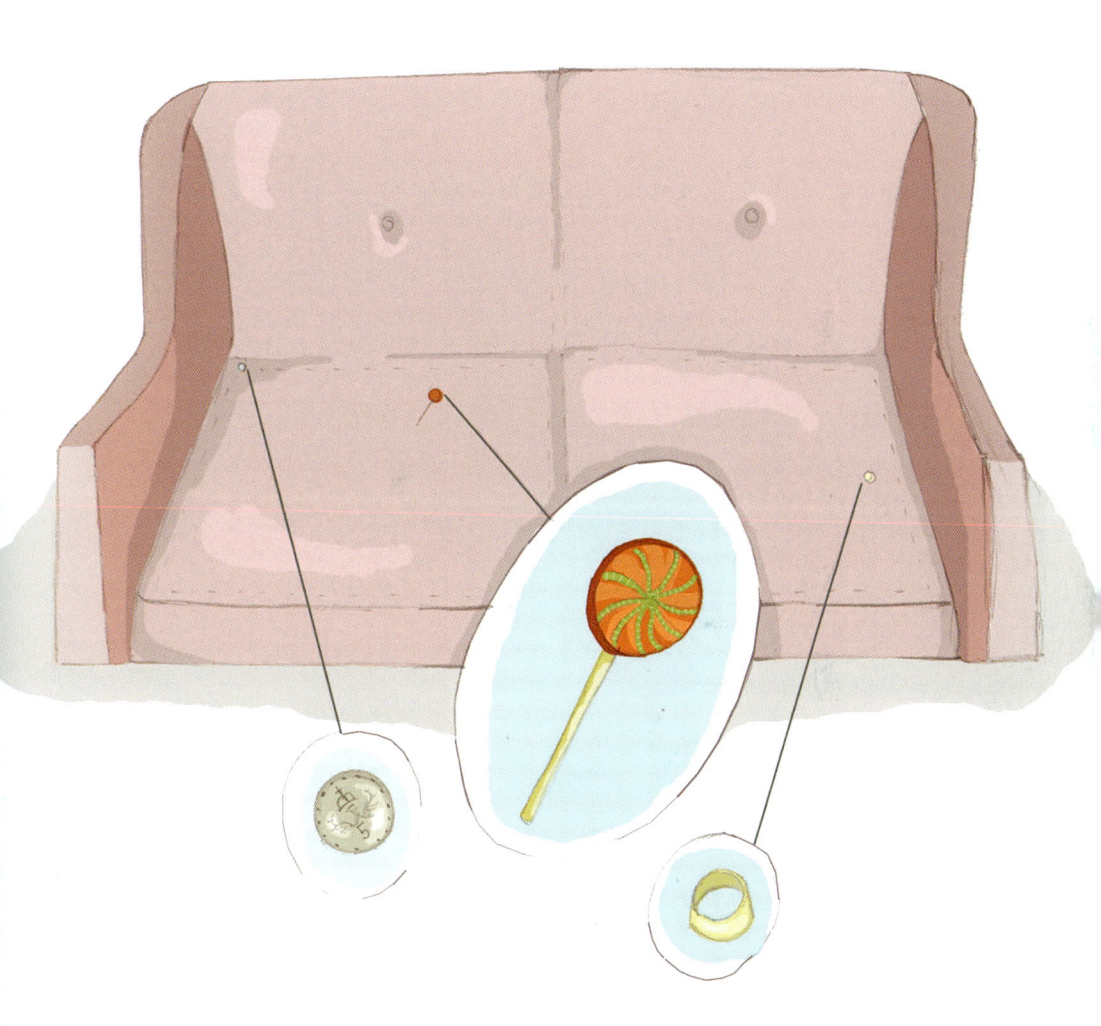

"Let's look in the toy trunk!"
said Adam.

It wasn't there.

But they did find
AN OVEN GLOVE,
A KEY AND
ONE OF ADAM'S RED SOCKS.

TOYS

"Let's look under
Mum and Dad's bed!"
Mariam said.

It wasn't there.

But they did find,
**A WOODEN SPOON,
DAD'S HAMMER
AND A STORY BOOK.**

Everyone thought very hard.
Then they realised something.
Dad asked Adam if he
remembered having the plane
with him when they came home.

Adam could not remember.

Mum knew what had happened.
When he found the toy train,
he forgot all about his plane
and **left it on the train!**

choo choo

Dad put him on his lap.

"DON'T WORRY," he said,
"I'm sure whoever found it
gave it to the lost property man,
LIKE YOU DID."

The next day, Mum took Adam
to see the lost property man.

"To prove this plane is yours,
tell me what is carved onto it?"
said the lost property man.

lost and found

"It says, **CAPTAIN ADAM!**"

"It sure does!
This is your plane Captain."
said the lost property man.

Adam was happy with his plane.
And he was happy he had given the toy
train to the lost property man.

If you enjoyed this book, you'll love Adam and the Tummy Monsters

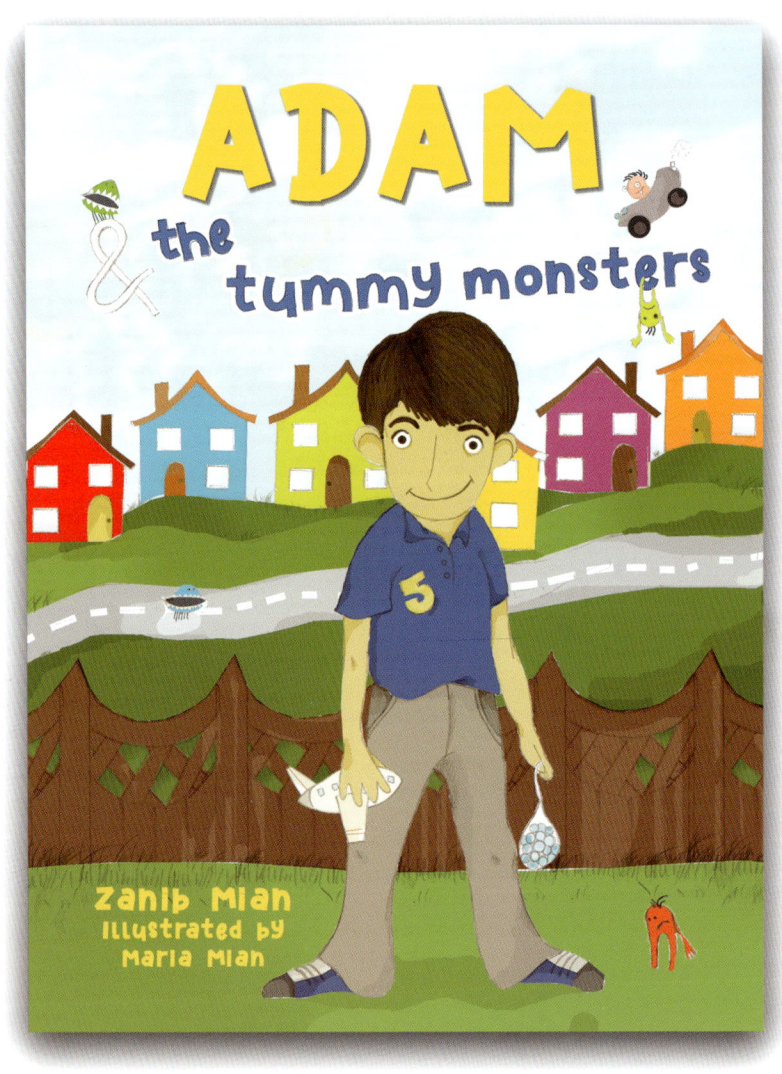